Roonie B. Moonie
Lost and Alone

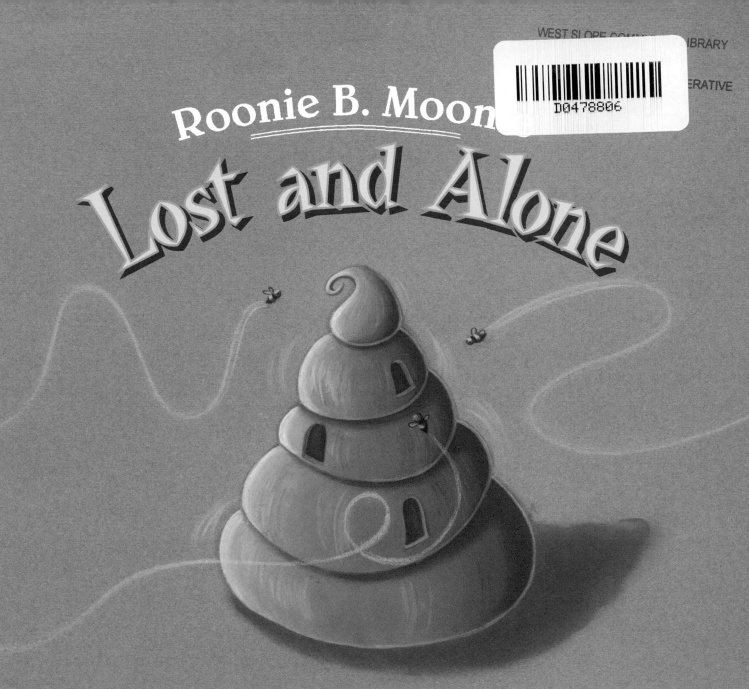

Janan Cain

ILLUMINATION Arts

PUBLISHING COMPANY, INC.
BELLEVUE, WASHINGTON

For my parents—
Jack & Nance Nagy
and George Koutny
who proudly displayed
my childhood paintings as if
they were masterpieces. —JC

For Roonie B. Moonie, today was a
perfect day. The sun was shining brightly, warming
his fuzzy shoulders, and the leaves in the garden were
dancing in the breeze, causing Roonie's propeller to
spin wildly. The garden was humming and alive with
mysterious sounds and scents, making it a great day
to do what he loved most…exploring!

Roonie was buzzing with excitement as he filled his backpack with all the necessary supplies— a flashlight, a magnifying glass and bee-noculars. He yearned to be a great explorer like his hero, Christopher Columblebee.

Mother B. Moonie, who often worried about her brave little bee, was careful to review the safety rules for being outside the hive. "Now Roonie, be sure to **stay in the open. Be extra careful around strangers.** And if you fly into trouble, remember to **stay calm, listen to your feelings and use your head.**"

Impatient (because he had heard these rules a thousand times before), Roonie eagerly flew off to begin his day of exploring. He buzzed around the garden until he became bored. Then, using his bee-noculars, he spotted an unusual object in the far distance that he had never seen before.

It was a mysterious hollow log. "Bee-eautiful!" shouted Roonie. "THIS definitely needs exploring!"

Zooming down for a closer look, Roonie found a hidden opening. In the back of his mind, he heard his mother's voice reminding him to **stay in the open.** "It looks safe enough," he thought. "I'll just take a quick peek."

Roonie zigged, and he zagged, until suddenly he was inside the log.

The little bee could see
nothing but blackness. He
smelled a damp, musty odor, like
the cellar of an old hive. "Anybody
here?" he called out nervously.

Roonie wondered if brave
explorers were ever frightened when
they were all alone in strange places.

Inside the log, all was quiet except
for the sound of his own breathing.
When Roonie realized that he
couldn't see the opening, he began
to feel really scared.

Trying **to calm himself,
Roonie took a deep breath.**
This helped him to think
clearly, and he remembered
his flashlight. But when he
turned it on, there were
big, scary strangers all
around him, and they
looked HUNGRY!

In a panic, Roonie
dropped his favorite flashlight
and didn't stop buzzing his little
wings until he was safely out of
the dark scary log.

"Whew! That was close," Roonie panted, as he landed on a
bumpy rock to look around the strange, unfamiliar place. Lost in
the thick brush, he had no idea how to get back to his hive.
"Where am I? Which way is home?" he sobbed. "What should
I do now?"

Roonie wanted to be home with his mother more than he had ever wanted anything before. So he dried his tears and took a few more deep breaths before starting to make his way through the tangled limbs and branches.

A brightly colored bird suddenly swooped down in front of him, blocking his way. "What's the matter, little bee? Are you lost?"

Although she didn't look dangerous, for some reason Roonie felt uncomfortable with this stranger.

"I'll be glad to help you! Come with me," urged the bird as she wrapped her strong wing around his fuzzy shoulders.

Once again, Roonie
remembered his mother's
voice saying, **"Trust your feelings
and use your head."** She had taught
him to stay away from anyone who made
him feel yucky or creepy, and that's just
how he felt now. "No, thank you!" Roonie
said bravely. "I don't want to go with you."
The bird seemed determined to change his
mind. "Come with me," she cooed, "and we'll find
some sweet nectar treats. Then I'll help you find
your mother."

Not feeling at all safe, Roonie raced toward
a nearby mushroom patch and crawled into
an opening where the bird could not follow.

Safely hidden, the worried little bee again took slow, deep breaths to calm his racing heart. He heard the soothing sound of flowing water, and it reminded him of the babbling brook that flowed past his bedroom window. "Maybe this will lead to my hive," he thought.

Leaving his protective shelter, Roonie found his way to the stream and jumped into a mushroom cap. Gently floating along, he daydreamed of a time exploring with his bee buddies when they had laughed so hard that their bellies hurt. The dream was so real, he could almost hear the laughter.

But it wasn't a dream! He really did hear laughter! A smiling mother ladybug was watching her children play in flower cups as they giggled with delight. "I wish my mom was here," Roonie thought sadly. "I know she would help someone who was lost."

Again he heard the echo of his mother's voice. "If you ever need help and can't find a Patrol Officer, ask a lady with small children."

Roonie took a deep breath and carefully approached the mother ladybug. "Ex-ex-excuse me," he said nervously, "My n-n-n-name is Roonie B. Moonie. I was exploring and got lost. Could you please call my mom and tell her where I am?"

"Of course I will call her," the ladybug replied kindly. As he recited the phone number, which he knew by heart, Roonie was happy that he had **trusted his feelings and used his head.**

Now that he felt safe, Roonie joined the little ladybugs swooping, looping, swirling, whirling, and swinging from the branches. His heart leapt when he spied his mother in the distance.

Unable to contain his excitement, Roonie hugged Mother B. Moonie tighter than ever before. "Oh Mom," he blurted, "I'm so happy to see you! I got lost inside a dark log and there were scary strangers all around me. And then a creepy bird wanted me to go with her, but I ran away and hid until I felt safe. When I finally found these nice ladybugs, **I trusted my feelings and used my head**, like you told me a thousand times…."

"I'm very proud of you, my brave honey bee," said his mother. "You did a great job keeping yourself safe. But when we get home, I'd like to know how you got into so much trouble in the first place."

As they flew home, Roonie couldn't help but wonder if tomorrow would be another perfect day... a perfect day for exploring.

A Note to Parents

All parents worry about the prospect of their children becoming lost in public places. *Roonie B. Moonie* teaches children about their internal warning systems that can help protect them if they are lost or in danger. The following recommendations may be helpful:

• Impress upon children the importance of remaining calm and thinking clearly if they do become lost.

• Help children learn to pay attention to how they feel about situations. Talk with them about instincts, how they sense when someone or something is unsafe or dangerous. Explore the feelings, thoughts, and emotions they experience when their bodies and minds give warnings.

• Children are taught to be obedient and respectful, but they should also know when it is right to defy adults. Be sure they understand that they don't always need to do what older people say. Help them practice saying "No!" forcefully.

• Most parents are embarrassed when children make scenes around other people. Be sure children know that sometimes their safety may depend on bringing as much attention to themselves as possible.

• Help children role play different situations in which adults try to take advantage of them. Teach them to be suspicious of anyone who makes them feel uncomfortable or won't take "no" for an answer. Practice this often.

• Teach children how to decide which adults are likely to be safe. Have them practice simple, clear ways to ask for help from strangers.

• Most parents admonish children to keep track of their belongings. Be sure they know when it is okay or even necessary to abandon their backpacks or favorite toys.

• Be sure young children and children with disabilities that affect communication skills wear identification bracelets with name, address, and telephone number. Children should learn this vital information by heart as early as possible. Try making this a game by creating a small jingle they can remember.

—Janan Cain

Recommended reading: *Protecting the Gift: Keeping Children and Teenagers Safe (and Parents Sane)* by Gavin de Becker.

Copyright © 2007 by Janan Cain

Library of Congress Cataloging-in-Publication Data

Cain, Janan, 10-11-1962
Lost and alone / written and illustrated by Janan Cain
p. cm.
Summary: Lost in a strange, unfamiliar place, an
adventurous young bee must follow his instincts and use his
head in order to avoid danger and keep himself safe.
ISBN-13 978-0-9740190-8-6
ISBN-10 0-9740190-8-9
[1. Strangers—Fiction. 2. Fear—Fiction.] I. Title.

2007937664

Published in the United States of America
Printed in Singapore by Tien Wah Press
Book Designed by Janan Cain

ILLUMINATION Arts

PUBLISHING COMPANY, INC.

P.O. Box 1865
Bellevue, WA 98009
Tel: 425-644-7185 • Fax: 425-644-9274
888-210-8216 (orders only)
liteinfo@illumin.com • www.illumin.com

Special thanks to:
John Cain
Carolyn Threadgill
Homer Henderson
John Thompson
Emma Roberts
Ruth Thompson
Arrieana Thompson
and
Kim Shealy